Ahoy there, kids! Ready to sing the
SpongeBob SquarePants theme song?
I can't hear you!
OOOOOOOOOOOOOOOOOH,
Who lives in a pineapple under the sea?
SpongeBob SquarePants!
Absorbent and yellow and porous is he.
SpongeBob SquarePants!
If nautical nonsense be something you wish.
SpongeBob SquarePants!
Then drop on the deck and flop like a fish.
SpongeBob SquarePants!
SpongeBob SquarePants!
SpongeBob SquarePants!
SpongeBob SquarePants!
Sponge— Bob,   Square— Pants!
Ah ha ha ha ah har har har

"Hold on, buddy!" yelled Patrick.

"I'm holding!" yelled SpongeBob.

The rocket shot out of the ocean and into the air.

"Good-bye, Bikini Bottom!" called SpongeBob.

The rocket went higher and higher into the sky.

Suddenly SpongeBob and Patrick began to float in the air.

"Help! Somebody get me down!" cried Patrick as he floated toward the top of the rocket. Then he turned upside down. "Help! Somebody get me up!"

SpongeBob looked out the window and saw the black sky filled with stars. Millions of stars. "We're in outer space!" he yelled.

If you purchased this book without a cover you should be
aware that this book is stolen property. It was reported as
"unsold and destroyed" to the publisher and neither the author
nor the publisher has received any payment for
this "stripped book."

Stephen Hillenburg

Based on the TV series *SpongeBob SquarePants*®
created by Stephen Hillenburg as seen on Nickelodeon®

SIMON SPOTLIGHT
An imprint of Simon & Schuster Children's Publishing Division
1230 Avenue of the Americas, New York, New York 10020

Manufactured in the United States of America

First Edition
2 4 6 8 10 9 7 5 3

ISBN 0-689-84193-0

Library of Congress Control Number 00-111806

by Steven Banks
illustrated by Clint Bond

Simon Spotlight/Nickelodeon

New York   London   Toronto   Sydney   Singapore

chapter one

SpongeBob SquarePants was running as fast as he could to Sandy Cheeks's house.

It was a beautiful day in Bikini Bottom and SpongeBob couldn't wait to see his friend. He wanted to show her a new karate move he had seen on TV.

"Hey, Sandy!" he yelled as he knocked on her door. "Open up, I . . ." Suddenly SpongeBob stopped knocking. He looked up and saw something next to Sandy's house. It made him forget all about the new karate move.

It was a rocket ship!

It was enormous. It was taller than Sandy's house. SpongeBob had to lean so far back to see the top that he fell over.

The rocket ship was painted red and silver. It had a point at the top and there were little windows on the side.

Sandy opened her front door. "Howdy, SpongeBob! How do you like my rocket ship?"

"Wow!" said SpongeBob.

"Let's go inside and I'll show you around," said Sandy, opening the door of the rocket ship.

"What are you going to do with it?" asked SpongeBob.

"I'm going to the moon!" said Sandy as they went inside.

SpongeBob's eyes opened wide. His heart began to beat fast. "The moon! Wow! Can I go?"

Sandy shook her head. "No way, SpongeBob! Remember what happened when you went with me to find The Lost City of Atlantis?"

"I forget," said SpongeBob.

"We found it and then you lost it!" said Sandy. "Besides, there's not enough room for you in my rocket ship."

"But I don't take up that much space," said SpongeBob as he squished himself down as small as he could get. "See?"

Sandy shook her head. "Sorry, SpongeBob. You can't go."

SpongeBob opened up a tiny drawer and squeezed inside it. "Wait, look! I can fit in here!" he called.

"I need that drawer for important scientific papers," said Sandy.

SpongeBob popped out of the drawer and looked around the rocket ship.

"How about in here?" asked SpongeBob as he jumped inside a test tube.

"I need that test tube, too," replied Sandy.

SpongeBob climbed inside a juice bottle. "I could stay in here," he said.

"No you can't!" cried Sandy. "SpongeBob, this is an important scientific mission! I don't have time for fun and games!"

"I do!" said SpongeBob as he popped out of the juice bottle.

"No games! And no stowaways either!" said Sandy.

SpongeBob saw a little cupboard with bars in the front. It looked like a little jail. He quickly climbed inside. "Fine! Put me in the brig! Lock me in irons! I don't mind! I just wanna go to the moon!"

Sandy pulled SpongeBob out. "That's my air vent, SpongeBob! I need that, too!"

SpongeBob got down on his knees. "Oh, please can I go to the moon? Can I? Can I? Please-please-please?"

Sandy sighed. She could always use an extra hand. And SpongeBob was fun to have around.

"All right!" she said. "You can ride in the cargo hold, as long as you don't act crazy!"

SpongeBob jumped up and began running around the rocket ship as fast as he could. "I'm going to the moon! I'm going to the moon! Moon ride! Moon ride! Fly me to the moon!"

Sandy grabbed him. "Hey! Be careful! Don't touch anything!"

SpongeBob immediately picked up a long tube that had a trigger and a net at the end. "Wow! Look at this popgun! Are we gonna go hunting aliens on the moon?"

"Aw, hush, silly!" said Sandy. "This is for

harvesting moon rocks. Come on, I'll show you."

They walked out of the rocket ship.

Sandy aimed the moon rock harvester at some faraway rocks. She pulled the trigger and little nets shot out and wrapped themselves around the rocks.

"See? That's how I can collect moon rock specimens," said Sandy. "I've even got an extra one that you can use."

"Great! But when we're done playing with the rocks, we can use it for some serious alien hunting, right?" asked SpongeBob.

Sandy sighed. "Aliens? Are you nuts? I've been to the moon. There are no aliens."

SpongeBob smiled and chuckled quietly. "Sandy, Sandy, Sandy. How can you be so unscientific? There's evidence of aliens all around us! How do you explain cooties?

Cowlicks? Ninety-nine-cent stores?"

Sandy shook her head. "SpongeBob, you don't know the first thing about outer space. Now go home and get some shut-eye. Be here tomorrow at the crack of dawn. And leave your crazy alien ideas behind!"

chapter two

SpongeBob immediately went home to his pineapple house and climbed into bed.

Gary, his pet snail, was on the floor next to SpongeBob's bed. Gary slept on a pile of newspapers just in case he had an accident. He wasn't pineapple-house-trained yet.

SpongeBob set his alarm clock for the crack of dawn. He tried to go to sleep, but he was so excited, it wasn't easy. He stared at his clock. He had *hours* to go before dawn.

"Hurry up!" he said to the alarm clock. "Go faster!"

The alarm clock paid no attention and kept on slowly ticking.

SpongeBob looked out his window. It was still dark. "Come on, crack of dawn—start cracking!"

Just then Patrick Star, SpongeBob's best friend, popped his head in the bedroom window. "Hiya, SpongeBob! I heard you were going to the moon with Sandy."

"I am. And I'm trying to go to sleep!" replied SpongeBob.

"I have to ask you a very important question," said Patrick as he climbed through the window. "Is Sandy's rocket safe from aliens?"

"There *are* no aliens," said SpongeBob. "Just ask Sandy . . . Little Miss Smarty-pants Scientist."

"Oh, really?" said Patrick as he held up a

brown paper bag. "Well, then I guess you won't be needing this can of Mr. Funny Ha-Ha's Alien Repellent Spray!"

"Mr. Funny Ha-Ha's Alien Repellent Spray!" cried SpongeBob, grabbing the bag. "Let me see that!"

SpongeBob pulled out a bright red spray can and read the label: "GUARANTEED TO KEEP ALL ALIENS AWAY! Where did you get this, Patrick?"

"I ordered it from a comic book," said Patrick proudly.

"Then aliens must be real!" exclaimed SpongeBob. "Let's go spray the rocket ship!"

chapter three

SpongeBob and Patrick quietly walked up to Sandy's rocket ship. It was late at night. Sandy was fast asleep in her bed.

"Okay, Patrick," said SpongeBob, "we'll just spray the outside of the rocket ship so it'll be safe from aliens, and then we'll go home."

Patrick ran up to the ship and saw a button marked PRESS THIS TO GET INSIDE ROCKET SHIP.

"Hey! We can get inside the rocket," said Patrick.

"No, we can't!" cried SpongeBob. "We're just spraying the outside and going home!"

"But all I have to do is push this," said Patrick as he pushed the button. The door opened—right on top of SpongeBob!

"Ouch!" cried SpongeBob.

"I did it! I opened it!" cried Patrick. "Let's go inside!"

Patrick ran inside and SpongeBob followed.

Inside there were flashing lights and levers and video screens and buttons everywhere.

"Holy sea cow!" cried Patrick. "This must be the control room!"

"Don't touch anything!" warned SpongeBob.

It was too late. Patrick was sitting in a chair in front of a video monitor. He was pushing buttons and pulling levers. He thought it was a video game.

"Look! I'm winning!" yelled Patrick.

"Cut it out!" said SpongeBob. "We can't hang around in here. This is Sandy's rocket. Stop playing!"

"I won *again!*" cried Patrick.

"Really?" asked SpongeBob, peering over Patrick's shoulder. "Can I have a turn? Gee, what game is that?"

Patrick shrugged. "I don't know. But let's see what these other things do!"

And then he reached up and pulled more levers and pushed more buttons.

"I like rockets!" said Patrick.

"Stop touching buttons!" yelled SpongeBob.

Just then Patrick saw a very interesting button.

"Not even *this* button?" asked Patrick. "I bet this is the one that starts the rocket."

SpongeBob shook his head. "Patrick, pardon me for pulling rank, but *I'm* the space traveler here. And I happen to know that the button to start the spaceship is right over here!"

SpongeBob pointed to a red button.

"That's not it!" said Patrick.

"Yes it is!" said SpongeBob.

"Prove it!" said Patrick.

"Okay!" said SpongeBob, and he pressed the button.

The rocket began to roar and shake and make a lot of noise.

"Uh-oh," said SpongeBob.

Patrick pointed at SpongeBob and laughed. "*You* started the rocket! *You* started the rocket! Ha! Ha! Ha!"

All the noise woke Sandy up. She saw her rocket ship blasting off—to the moon!

She sat up in bed and yelled, "SPONGEBOB!"

chapter four

SpongeBob and Patrick were holding onto one another as the rocket ship shook, rattled, and rolled.

"Hold on, buddy!" yelled Patrick.

"I'm holding!" yelled SpongeBob.

The rocket shot out of the ocean and into the air.

"Good-bye, Bikini Bottom!" called SpongeBob.

The rocket went higher and higher into the sky.

Suddenly SpongeBob and Patrick began to float in the air.

"Help! Somebody get me down!" cried Patrick as he floated toward the top of the rocket. Then he turned upside down. "Help! Somebody get me up!"

SpongeBob looked out the window and saw the black sky filled with stars. Millions of stars. "We're in outer space!" he yelled.

SpongeBob and Patrick started to have fun, turning somersaults and floating in the air.

"I'm a bird!" said Patrick.

"I'm a balloon!" cried SpongeBob.

The rocket ship was headed right for the moon. Exactly as Sandy had programmed it.

But SpongeBob and Patrick weren't paying attention to where the rocket ship was going. They were too busy flying and floating.

Patrick kept banging into the walls and

hitting buttons. He hit so many buttons, he changed the direction of the rocket ship. The rocket ship went right around the moon and headed back toward Earth!

SpongeBob and Patrick didn't notice. They were having too much fun.

☆

Meanwhile, back in Bikini Bottom, Sandy was strapping on a rocket jet pack. It allowed her to lift off into space all by herself.

As she tightened the straps, she shook her head. "Sometimes that SpongeBob is as dumb as a sack of peanuts! What the heck did he think he was doing, taking off in my rocket? I better get up there on the moon before he gets into more trouble!"

Sandy blasted off in her rocket jet pack, never seeing the rocket carrying SpongeBob and Patrick as it splashed back into the water.

chapter five

As the rocket ship came out of space, SpongeBob and Patrick stopped floating and fell to the floor.

"I'm not a bird anymore!" said Patrick.

"We must be landing on the moon!" exclaimed SpongeBob.

"All right!" yelled Patrick.

SpongeBob and Patrick put on their space suits and filled them with water so they wouldn't dry out.

"Patrick, prepare to walk on the moon!" proclaimed SpongeBob.

"Aye, aye, Captain!" replied Patrick.

SpongeBob carefully opened the door of the rocket ship. They popped their heads out and saw . . . Squidward's tiki house and SpongeBob's pineapple house and Patrick's rock.

"Wow . . . the moon sure looks a lot like home," said Patrick.

"Good!" said SpongeBob. "We won't feel homesick."

SpongeBob carefully stepped out onto the sand. "This is one small step for a sponge, one giant leap for spongekind!"

Just then Gary, SpongeBob's pet snail, came crawling by.

Patrick pointed. "Hey, look! It's Gary!"

"Meow," said Gary.

"Come here, Gary!" cried Patrick as he started to run toward him.

SpongeBob grabbed Patrick. "Stop! Don't go near him!"

"Why not?" asked Patrick.

"This is all a trick!" warned SpongeBob. "The aliens are projecting our memories onto the environment! They want us to think this is Bikini Bottom, but it's *really* the moon. They're trying to confuse us!"

Patrick scratched his head. "You mean to say they've taken what we thought we think and made us think we thought our thoughts we've been thinking are thoughts we think we thought?"

SpongeBob nodded. "I couldn't have said it better! But we're not going to fall for it!"

SpongeBob aimed the moon rock harvester popgun at Gary. "You who are not Gary, but pretend to be Gary, prepare to be harvested!"

SpongeBob pushed the button on the moon rock harvester. *ZAP!*

Suddenly Gary was wrapped up in a net.

SpongeBob grinned. "Now what do you have to say for yourself, Mr. Alien?"

"Meow," said Gary.

"You got 'em, SpongeBob! What a shot!" cried Patrick. "Boy, is Sandy gonna be proud!"

SpongeBob turned pale. "Sandy! Oh, no! I forgot all about her! She's going to be really mad at us for stealing her rocket!"

SpongeBob didn't know what to do. He couldn't stand the idea of Sandy being mad at him. He was trying to think of something he could say or do when Gary meowed again.

"That's it!" said SpongeBob. "Sandy won't hate us when I bring her back a real live alien! Or two! Or three! Or four! Or more! She'll love me! Come, Patrick! Let the alien harvesting begin!"

chapter six

SpongeBob raced across the sand toward Squidward's house.

Patrick followed and began to yell excitedly, "Oh, boy! Alien hunting! Alien hunting!"

"Quiet, Patrick!" whispered SpongeBob. "We can't let the aliens know we're on to them."

SpongeBob then spoke loudly so anyone nearby could hear. "Oh, yeah! *Alien Hunting.* That was a great TV show! Amazing special effects!"

SpongeBob motioned for Patrick to follow him to Squidward's front door. "Hey, Patrick!" he shouted. "Let's go visit our good old friend Squidward and see what he's up to!"

SpongeBob knocked on the door.

No one answered.

They quietly pushed the door open and went inside.

"Make sure your alien harvester popgun is ready to go," whispered SpongeBob as they walked into Squidward's bedroom.

Squidward was asleep in his bed. His four little bunny slippers were next to his bed on the floor.

"That is one ugly alien," said SpongeBob.

"It's disgusting!" added Patrick.

Squidward was dreaming and talking in his sleep, "Uh . . . no . . . Grandma . . . don't take away my clarinet . . . I'll be a good squid."

SpongeBob and Patrick walked right up to Squidward's bed and looked down at him as he slept.

"It's even uglier up close," whispered SpongeBob. "Let's begin the alien examination."

SpongeBob pulled back Squidward's blanket. Squidward was wearing a nightshirt with little bears and ducks on it.

Patrick looked closer. "Look! There's something underneath the alien!"

SpongeBob saw something red and rubbery under Squidward's body.

"I think I'm going to be sick!" said Patrick.

SpongeBob pulled it out. It was only Squidward's rubber hot-water bottle. He used it at night to keep himself warm.

But SpongeBob thought it was something else. He held it up to Patrick. "Do you know what this is?" he asked.

"It's stinky!" replied Patrick.

"No," said SpongeBob. "It's an egg sack!"

"It's a stinky egg sack," said Patrick.

SpongeBob continued. "This disgusting alien creature has laid an egg, and if I'm correct, it is filled with baby aliens!"

"Now I *know* I'm gonna be sick!" cried Patrick.

SpongeBob held the hot-water bottle up to the lamp next to Squidward's bed. The light shone behind the hot-water bottle and showed the silhouette of SpongeBob's two hands.

"Twins!" cried SpongeBob. "Horrible, disgusting, evil alien twins!"

Just then Squidward turned over and one of his tentacles landed on Patrick's face.

SPLAT!

"Help! Get this thing off of me!" screamed Patrick.

SpongeBob quickly reached up to pull Squidward's tentacle off of Patrick's face.

It was stuck!

"Don't let the alien get me, SpongeBob!" cried Patrick.

"I won't!" yelled SpongeBob.

With all the noise and yelling, Squidward woke up. "Patrick! SpongeBob! What are you doing in my bedroom? Give me back my tentacle!" Squidward pulled his tentacle off Patrick's face.

"The evil, disgusting thing is awake!" cried SpongeBob.

"Hey! Watch who you're calling evil and disgusting!" yelled Squidward.

"Let's capture the little phony!" said SpongeBob.

"Get away from me!" yelled Squidward as he jumped out of his bed.

Squidward tried to run away, but Patrick tackled him.

"Ouch!" cried Squidward.

"Hold him, Patrick!" yelled SpongeBob as he got his moon rock harvester ready and aimed it at Squidward.

"SpongeBob!" cried a terrified Squidward. "What in the name of Neptune are you doing?"

"What any other patriotic Bikini Bottom citizen would do!" declared SpongeBob.

ZAP!

chapter seven

Mr. Krabs, SpongeBob's boss, and owner of the Krusty Krab, was out taking his sea snake for a late-night walk.

Mr. Krabs was thinking of all the money he had made that day. Suddenly he heard a strange noise and saw SpongeBob and Patrick coming out of Squidward's house. They were carrying a very mysterious-looking bag.

"Ahoy there, lads! Up a bit late to be playing pirate, aren't ya? Got yourselves a new mate?"

asked Mr. Krabs with a laugh.

SpongeBob nudged Patrick. "It's another alien! Let's get him!"

They both pulled out their popguns and aimed them at Mr. Krabs.

Mr. Krabs was terrified. "No! Don't shoot me!"

SpongeBob got him in his sights. "Ready, aim—"

Mr. Krabs held up his pincers. "Wait a minute! On second thought, go ahead and shoot me! Just don't take me sweet, lovely money!"

"We don't want your money, moon man!" said SpongeBob.

Mr. Krabs breathed a sigh of relief. "Well, that be the best news I've heard all day!"

"We want you!" shouted Patrick.

ZAP!

And the next thing he knew, Mr. Krabs was caught in a net.

"SpongeBob!" yelled Mr. Krabs. "If you don't let me out of here, you'll never flip another Krabby Patty as long as you live!"

"Nice try, alien!" said SpongeBob.

☆

Meanwhile Sandy had landed on the moon. She looked and looked and looked, but there was no SpongeBob and no rocket ship.

"Where did that knucklehead go?" she wondered. "He must've gone back to Bikini Bottom. I'd better get back there too."

She pushed the button on her rocket jet pack and blasted off for home.

☆

Down in Bikini Bottom, SpongeBob and Patrick went back to the rocket ship. They tossed the nets with Squidward and Mr. Krabs into the cargo hold with Gary.

"Ouch!" cried Squidward.

"Ow!" yelled Mr. Krabs.

"Meow," said Gary.

SpongeBob stared at the three of them. "Look at them! Squirming around in there like a bunch of ugly, disgusting aliens!"

"They're gross!" said Patrick.

SpongeBob closed the hatch. "It's a tough job, but someone has to do it! And that someone is us! We have a mission, Patrick. It's time for an alien roundup!"

☆

SpongeBob and Patrick went to Mrs. Puff's Boating School.

Mrs. Puff was correcting papers at her desk when she looked up and saw them coming into her room.

"SpongeBob SquarePants! Patrick Star!" said Mrs. Puff. "What are you doing here so late?"

SpongeBob sneered. "We'll ask the questions here, Mrs. Puff! If that *is* your real name, and I happen to know it *isn't!*"

Mrs. Puff angrily stood up. "SpongeBob! You are going to sit in the corner and think about what you just said!"

"School's out, sister!" yelled SpongeBob.

Mrs. Puff started to scream but it was too late. *ZAP!*

As they dragged her out of the schoolroom in her net, Mrs. Puff yelled, "This is going on your permanent record, SpongeBob!"

☆

SpongeBob and Patrick continued to round up everyone in Bikini Bottom.

They found Pearl, Mr. Krabs's daughter, at the Whale Watchers Mall. She was so big, being a whale, that they had to use six nets to capture her!

"Excuse me!" she complained. "But this net does *not* go with my outfit!"

☆

Next they captured Plankton, the owner of Plankton's Chum Bucket and the smallest resident of Bikini Bottom. He was trying to sneak into the Krusty Krab to steal a Krabby Patty.

"At last I will have the secret recipe for Krabby Patties and the world will be mine!" Plankton bellowed.

"Not so fast!" cried SpongeBob.

"You're an alien and you're going down!" said Patrick.

"Ha! You'll never get me!" yelled Plankton.

ZAP!

"You got me," said Plankton sadly.

chapter eight

Soon the entire population of Bikini Bottom was wrapped up in nets. SpongeBob and Patrick were pushing them into the cargo hold of the rocket ship. It was getting very crowded.

"SpongeBob, we've got a problem," said Patrick. "They can't all fit in the rocket ship!"

"Just push harder!" said SpongeBob. "We must get all of the aliens!"

"We're not *aliens!*" screamed Squidward from inside his net.

"Hah! That's what they *all* say," said SpongeBob.

"Of course we're *all* saying it! It's true!" roared Mr. Krabs.

"I have to get back to the mall!" cried Pearl.

"I have test papers to correct!" said Mrs. Puff.

"Give me liberty or give me the recipe to Krabby Patties!" screamed Plankton.

"Don't listen to them, Patrick," warned SpongeBob. "They're just trying to confuse us with their evil alien ways!"

They were pushing the last "alien" into the rocket ship when suddenly they heard a noise coming from above.

"Look, SpongeBob!" cried Patrick. "It's Sandy!"

Sandy was floating down toward them. "SpongeBob! What are y'all doing? I can't turn my back on you for two whole seconds without

you causin' a heap of trouble!"

"Help us, Sandy!" yelled Squidward.

Sandy landed on the ocean floor and looked into the cargo hold. She saw everyone from Bikini Bottom wrapped up in nets.

"What the heck is going on here?" asked Sandy. "Bagging up all your friends and neighbors just like they were a fresh crop of hickory-smoked sausages! You done turned my little science experiment into a disaster! You ought to be ashamed of yourselves!"

SpongeBob aimed his alien harvester popgun at Sandy.

"Nice try, Ms. Alien, but I'm not falling for it!" said SpongeBob.

"Are you sure that's not the real Sandy?" asked Patrick.

"Zap now. Ask questions later," said SpongeBob.

Sandy glared at SpongeBob. "Why are you aiming that moon rock harvester at me?"

"Because *you* are an alien," said SpongeBob. "And it's not a moon rock harvester, it's an alien harvester!"

ZAP!

And then Sandy was in a net, just like the others. SpongeBob and Patrick tossed her into the cargo hold.

"Aliens!" exclaimed Sandy. "Is that what this is all about? You think we're all aliens?"

SpongeBob pushed the button to close the cargo door hatch.

The door slowly closed as Sandy kept yelling, "This isn't the moon! You're still in Bikini—"

The door closed. Neither SpongeBob nor Patrick heard her.

SpongeBob shook his head. "Just goes to show you, Patrick, you can't trust anyone!

Anybody could be an alien! Even . . ."

SpongeBob looked at Patrick suspiciously.

"Patrick! You were an alien all along!" said SpongeBob.

"I was?" asked Patrick.

"And you didn't even tell me!" said SpongeBob.

SpongeBob aimed his zapper at Patrick. Patrick aimed his zapper at SpongeBob. "Not so fast! It's not you that's got me . . . it's . . . it's me that's got me!"

And with that, Patrick turned his popgun around and zapped himself right in the face, wrapping himself in a net.

"Help! I'm an alien!" cried Patrick.

chapter nine

SpongeBob threw Patrick in the cargo hold. Then he got in the rocket ship and raced up to the control room.

SpongeBob smiled as he pushed the BLAST OFF button. "Boy, I can't wait to see the look on Sandy's face when I get back to Bikini Bottom with all these aliens! She's gonna think I'm the greatest guy in the world!"

SpongeBob set the controls for extra super fast.

The rocket ship zoomed through space, carrying its cargo of confused sea creatures.

"Bikini Bottom here we come!" he yelled.

When the rocket ship landed, SpongeBob ran out and yelled, "Hey, Sandy! I'm back! Come see what I found!"

He stopped.

He looked around.

He didn't see his pineapple house or Squidward's tiki house or Patrick's rock or even the Krusty Krab.

All he saw were craters and rocks and more craters and rocks.

Wow, he thought to himself, Bikini Bottom sure has changed.

And then SpongeBob looked up in the sky and saw . . . the Earth.

"Uh-oh," said SpongeBob.

"SPONGEBOB!" yelled Sandy, Squidward,

Patrick, Mr. Krabs, Mrs. Puff, Pearl, and all the other Bikini Bottom residents.

SpongeBob opened the cargo hold.

"Uh . . . there seems to have been a little mistake," said SpongeBob.

"Get us out of here!" shouted Sandy.

SpongeBob let everybody out of the nets.

"What do you have to say for yourself, SpongeBob?" asked Squidward.

"I'm sorry," cried SpongeBob. "It was all my fault! I was blinded by science! You all go back home. I'll stay on the moon. That will be my punishment! Banished from Bikini Bottom forever!"

"Sounds good to me!" said Squidward.

"Aw heck, we can't leave SpongeBob here," said Sandy. "Bikini Bottom wouldn't be the same without him."

"I agree!" said SpongeBob.

And so they all blasted off for home.

Sandy steered the rocket ship back toward Earth.

"SpongeBob, I hope you learned your lesson," said Sandy.

"Oh, I have," said SpongeBob. "Never go into your friend's rocket ship without her permission. Never fly to the moon. And *never* catch all your friends in nets because you think they are aliens."

"That's pretty close, I reckon," she said.

"So, Sandy?" asked SpongeBob. "Where are we going next? Mars? Venus? Pluto? . . ."

"Settle down, SpongeBob. I can't concentrate!"

". . . Jupiter, Saturn, Uranus?" SpongeBob continued.

"I know exactly where *you're* going," said Sandy.

"Where?" asked SpongeBob excitedly. "Will I get to catch aliens?"

ZAP!

And with that, Sandy shot her popgun at SpongeBob, wrapped him in a net, and put him in the cargo hold.

"Oh, no!" screamed Patrick. "SpongeBob is an alien!"

Sandy shook her head.

It was going to be a long trip back to Bikini Bottom.

about the author

Steven Banks is a writer and actor who plays a number of musical instruments and writes scripts and songs for children's television. When he was a kid, Steven and his family watched every single lift-off of the Mercury Space Program and once even made what he says was "a very cool space capsule in my closet!" He lives in Glendale, California.